EVERYTHING SPORTS

EVERYTHING GYMNASTICS

CHRÖS MCDOUGALL

SportsZone
An Imprint of Abdo Publishing
abdobooks.com

abdobooks.com

Published by Abdo Publishing, a division of ABDO, PO Box 398166, Minneapolis, Minnesota 55439.

Printed in the United States of America, North Mankato, Minnesota.
052024
092024

THIS BOOK CONTAINS RECYCLED MATERIALS

Cover Photos: Petr Toman/Shutterstock Images (Simone Biles); Melissa J. Perenson/Cal Sport Media/AP Images (Olivia Dunne); Real Sports Photos/Shutterstock Images (background)
Interior Photos: Dan Morley/Hulton Archive/Getty Images, 4–5; Bettmann/Getty Images, 6, 21; Aric Becker/Icon Sportswire/Getty Images, 9; Universal History Archive/Universal Images Group/Getty Images, 11; RDB/ullstein bild/Getty Images, 13; Laurence Griffiths/Getty Images Sport/Getty Images, 14–15; Robert Gautheir/Los Angeles Times/Getty Images, 17; Horstmüller/ullstein bild/Getty Images, 18; Wally McNamee/Corbis Historical/Getty Images, 23; Emmanuel Dunand/AFP/Getty Images, 25, 39; ullstein bild/Getty Images, 26–27; David Madison/Getty Images Sport/Getty Images, 29; Kyodo/AP Images, 30–31; Tim Clayton/Corbis Sport/Getty Images, 32–33; An Yuan/China News Service/VCG/Getty Images, 35; Loren Vu/DPPI-SIPA/AP Images, 36–37; Kyle Okita/Cal Sport Media/ZUMA Press Wire/AP Images, 40–41; Jayne Kamin-Oncea/Getty Images Sport/Getty Images, 43; Melissa J. Perenson/Cal Sport Media/AP Images, 44–45; Doug Pensinger/Getty Images Sport/Getty Images, 46–47; Rebecca Blackwell/AP Images, 49; Nhat V. Meyer/San Jose Mercury News/MCT/Abaca Press/Alamy, 51; Jean Catuffe/Getty Images Sport/Getty Images, 52–53; Olivier Morin/AFP/Getty Images, 55; Foto Olimpik/NurPhoto/Getty Images, 56–57; Loic Venance/AFP/Getty Images, 58–59; Naomi Baker/Getty Images Sport/Getty Images, 61

Editor: Charlie Beattie
Series Designer: Karli Kruse

Library of Congress Control Number: 2023949388
Publisher's Cataloging-in-Publication Data
Names: McDougall, Chrös, author.
Title: Everything gymnastics / by Chrös McDougall
Description: Minneapolis, Minnesota: Abdo Publishing, 2025 | Series: Everything sports | Includes online resources and index.
Identifiers: ISBN 9781098293581 (lib. bdg.) | ISBN 9798384912859 (ebook)
Subjects: LCSH: Gymnastics--Juvenile literature. | Gymnasts--Juvenile literature. | Gymnastics injuries--Juvenile literature. | Artistic gymnastics--Juvenile literature. | Gymnastics coaches--Juvenile literature. | Gymnastics--Training--Juvenile literature. | Gymnastics--Rules--Juvenile literature. | Sports--Juvenile literature.
Classification: DDC 796.41--dc23

TABLE OF CONTENTS

CHAPTER ONE

THE PERFECT 10

From a running start, Nadia Comăneci seemed to float over the low bar like a butterfly. The Romanian gymnast, just 14 years old, tapped that low bar and then grabbed on to the high bar, swinging up to begin her routine. Fans at the 1976 Olympic Games in Montreal, Canada, looked on eagerly as the teenage star moved swiftly through her skills.

With straight legs and pointed toes, Comăneci swung from bar to bar. Twice she pressed her lower body against the low bar while holding on to the high bar. The skills seemed to flow together with ease. To end the routine, Comăneci began with a handstand atop the high bar. Then she swung down and drove her hips into the low bar. Using her momentum, Comăneci whipped around the bar by her waist and then soared into the air with her arms spread. Finally, she landed softly onto the mat and quickly saluted the judges.

Nadia Comăneci's graceful routines captivated fans throughout the 1976 Olympics in Montreal, Canada.

Everyone watching knew it was a special performance. But how special was it? When her score finally appeared, it read "1.00." No one was sure what to think. Such a score was impossibly low. Then the reality set in. Comăneci had actually scored 10.00. The scoreboard simply was not equipped to display four numbers—and for good reason.

Comăneci retired from competition in 1984 having won five Olympic gold medals, three silvers, and one bronze.

No gymnast had ever achieved a perfect score at the Olympics or World Championships.

Fans were instantly struck by what they'd seen. With that score, the judges were saying that Comăneci had performed ideal gymnastics. There was nothing to improve. And as the Montreal Games went on, Comăneci added six more perfect 10s. Three more came on the uneven bars. The three others were on the balance beam. The scores helped elevate Comăneci to five medals, including three golds. That performance also shot the young gymnast into superstardom.

MODERN SCORING

In 2006, a new scoring system was introduced for elite gymnastics. This marked the end of the perfect 10. Now gymnasts receive separate scores for difficulty and execution. Each skill in a routine is assigned a point value. The difficulty score, or D score, simply adds these up. It is "open ended," meaning there is no maximum score. The execution score, or E score, grades how well the gymnast performs those skills. The highest possible E score is 10.0. The D and E scores are then added together to determine a routine's final score.

For most of gymnastics history, routines were judged on the 10-point scale. After Comăneci's breakthrough, many other gymnasts achieved the score. Some fans argued that it was happening too often. Nonetheless, fans embraced the score. It was simple to understand. In many ways,

GYM SLAMS

In women's college gymnastics, a gymnast who records a perfect 10 in all four events achieves a Gym Slam. Jade Carey, a US Olympian competing for Oregon State, joined the club in 2023. That made her the 13th woman to earn a Gym Slam. But no one can match Trinity Thomas. With at least five 10s on each event, she holds the record with five Gym Slams.

the "perfect 10" became synonymous with the sport.

The perfect score no longer exists in elite gymnastics—the sport's top level, and the one at which Olympians compete. Instead, the sport has used an "open-ended" scoring system since 2006. The new scoring was supposed to be fairer. It was also designed to be more accurate.

Yet, the iconic perfect 10 lives on at other levels of the sport. Today it is most closely connected with college gymnastics. College fans eagerly follow each routine, hoping to see the special score. And the sport's biggest stars often deliver. Trinity Thomas arrived at the University of Florida after a decorated career at the elite level. Her stellar gymnastics quickly became a hit. And in her last meet, the 2023 college national championships, she scored her 28th perfect 10, joining a three-way tie for the most ever. A half century after Comăneci, the perfect 10 was still captivating fans and creating gymnastics superstars.

Trinity Thomas had 12 perfect 10s on floor exercise, six on the balance beam, and five each on the vault and uneven bars while at Florida.

CHAPTER TWO

ANCIENT HISTORY

Today's gymnasts captivate fans with their incredible athleticism, high-flying acrobatics, and awesome strength. Gymnastics is one of the most popular sports in the Olympic Games. But the sport has gone through many changes over the years.

Gymnastics was included in the first modern Olympic Games in 1896. However, its origins are much older. Young men in ancient Greece were performing gymnastics exercises more than 2,000 years earlier. These exercises included various physical challenges that took place in a space called a gymnasium. They included tumbling, but also activities such as running, swimming, and weightlifting. Gymnastics was meant to help the men prepare for war.

Gymnastics as we know it today began during the early 1800s. A German educator named Friedrich Ludwig Jahn created a gymnastics club to improve the physical fitness of his countrymen. Among his inventions were the balance beam, pommel horse, parallel bars, and high bar. His exercises grew in popularity across Germany, and eventually

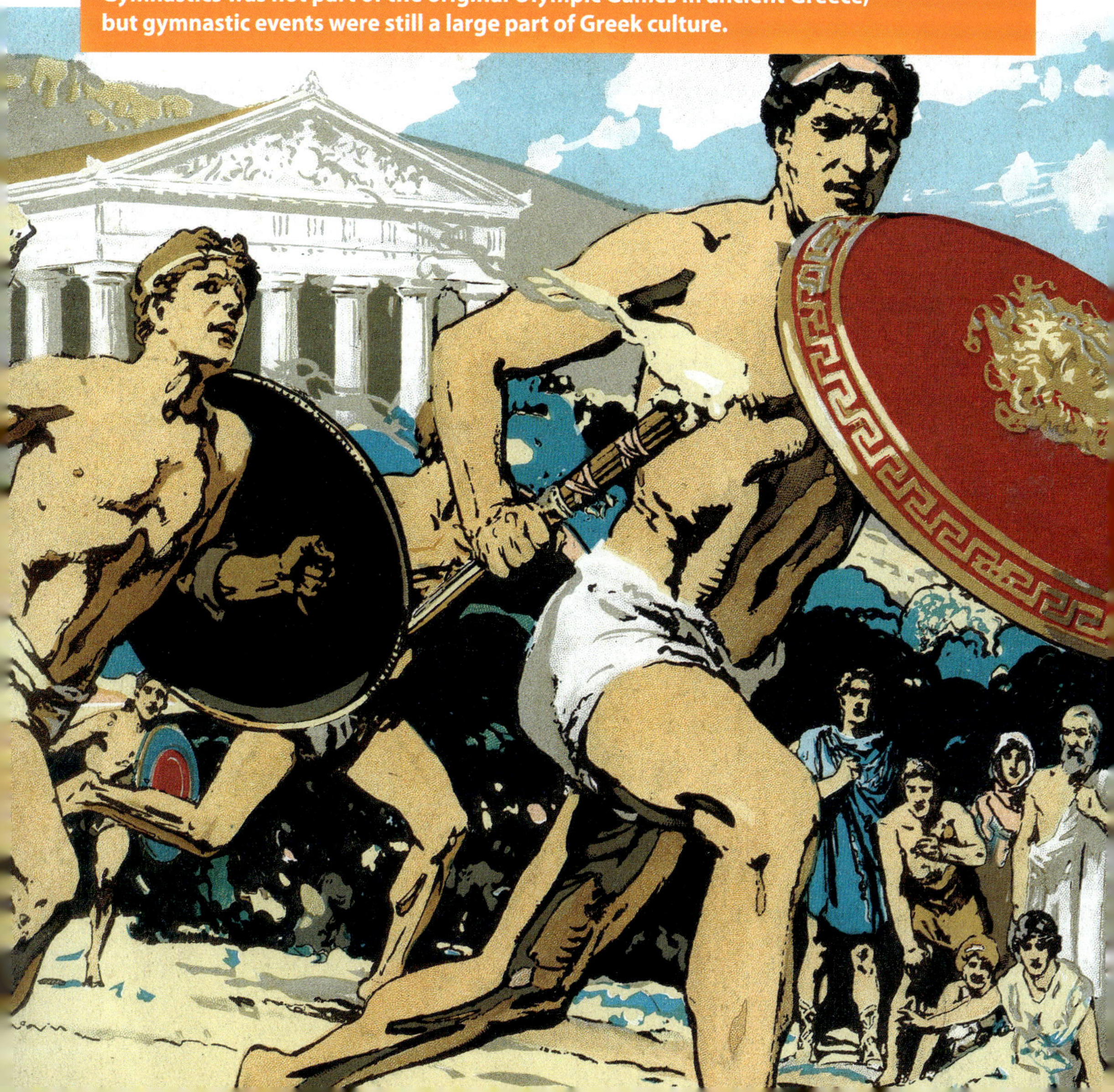

Gymnastics was not part of the original Olympic Games in ancient Greece, but gymnastic events were still a large part of Greek culture.

in other countries, too. Jahn became known as the Father of Gymnastics.

In 1881, the International Gymnastics Federation (FIG) formed. It's still the sport's governing body. Fifteen years later, the first Olympic gymnastics program in 1896 included eight events for men. A women's gymnastics event was added to the Games in 1928.

The Olympic gymnastics program has changed over the years. In four early Olympics, male gymnasts competed in rope climbing. Men's club swinging and side horse are among other events that had brief stints in the Games. The sport began standardizing its events in 1928. However, it wasn't until 1960 that the now familiar Olympic program was adopted. Since then, men have competed across eight events, while women have six.

THE WORLD CHAMPIONSHIPS

The first World Championships for men were held in 1903. Women's events were added in 1934. Originally held every two years, the event later changed to a four-year cycle like the Olympics before going back to every other year. It's now held in every non-Olympic year. The World Championships typically has the same basic format as the Olympics. However, there is no team competition in the first World Championships after an Olympics.

One of the biggest changes in the Olympic era has been the approach to women. Early on, many

Takashi Ono of Japan was one of the superstars of men's gymnastics in the 1950s and 1960s.

believed sports were too strenuous and unladylike for women. The FIG eventually began including women's events. However, the sport was designed to "align with traditional female values," rewarding qualities such as flexibility and grace. These are still part of women's gymnastics. Yet today's female gymnasts also perform daring, powerful, athletic feats just like the men.

CHAPTER THREE

ALL-AROUND GYMNASTICS

In a gymnastics meet, athletes perform routines on different apparatuses. Each apparatus is designed to test different qualities. Some require great strength or coordination. Others emphasize balance, flexibility, endurance, or agility. To succeed, a gymnast must possess all these qualities.

Women compete on four apparatuses. They are the balance beam, floor exercise, uneven bars, and vault. The balance beam is often called the most difficult event. Gymnasts must perform jumps, turns, poses, and other skills on a beam that's just 4 inches (10 cm) wide. Their movements must be precise to avoid falling off.

Gymnasts can be most expressive on floor exercise. This is a performance to music on a flat, square area that is 39 feet (12 meters) long on each side. A great floor exercise performer is both powerful and graceful. Springs under the floor help the gymnasts execute acrobatic jumps

Great Britain's Georgia-Mae Fenton performs a daring move on the balance beam at a competition in 2022.

and other tumbling. But dance elements bring out the gymnast's artistry.

Some of the most thrilling routines are seen on the uneven bars. One bar is 7.8 feet (2.4 m) off the ground. The other is 5.4 feet (1.65 m) high. Using their upper-body strength, gymnasts seamlessly swing between the bars. In daring release moves, they let go of a bar, perform a skill, and grab the bar again. The routine ends with a high-flying dismount.

TEAM GYMNASTICS

The Olympics and World Championships include men's and women's team events. The format has changed over the years. In 2024, the Olympics returned to five-gymnast teams. In qualifying, four gymnasts perform on each event. The best three scores count toward the team score. But there is no room for error in the team final. That's because only three gymnasts compete on each event, and all three scores are used.

Vault is the power event. Gymnasts build up speed on a runway. Then they launch themselves off a springboard and onto the vaulting table. Pushing off the table with their hands, the gymnast then performs a series of twists and flips before landing on the mat.

Men's gymnastics also includes floor exercise and vault. One difference is that men's floor exercise is not performed to music. As a result, their routines emphasize the gymnastics skills more than artistry. The other men's events are high bar, parallel bars, pommel horse, and still rings.

Gymnasts pick up speed for their vaults by sprinting down an 82-foot (25-m) runway.

Sawao Katō of Japan won the men's all-around competition at both the 1968 Olympics in Mexico City, Mexico, and the 1972 Games in Munich, West Germany.

The high bar, also called horizontal bar, is roughly 9 feet (2.75 m) off the ground. Exciting routines combine powerful swings, intricate turns, and giant release moves. The parallel bars are 6.4 feet (1.95 m) high and usually around 20 inches (51 cm) apart. Gymnasts move around the bars by swinging. Holds such as handstands demonstrate upper-body strength.

The pommel horse is a leather form with two wooden handles, called pommels. Gymnasts hold themselves up using their hands. They must constantly swing their legs in a circular motion around the horse to avoid falling off. The still rings test a gymnast's upper-body strength and control. The gymnast holds himself in various positions while grasping two wooden rings. Some moves also require swinging.

Gymnasts can specialize in certain events. The Olympics and World Championships have stand-alone finals on each apparatus. However, the most prestigious gymnastics competition is the all-around. This is when gymnasts perform on every apparatus. Those scores are then combined to determine the winner. The all-around champion is the person who has best mastered the qualities of a great gymnast.

CHAPTER FOUR
ICONIC WOMEN

For a half century, Soviet star Larisa Latynina set the standard in women's gymnastics. Latynina made her Olympic debut in 1956. By the end of her final games in 1964, she owned 18 medals—and half of them were gold. That stood as the Olympic record until swimmer Michael Phelps won a 19th medal in 2012.

Yet, Latynina's gymnastics would look almost totally out of place to fans today. Her skills were more balletic and less acrobatic. Even she agreed. "What we did is not comparable to what modern gymnasts do," Latynina said in 2021.

The sport evolves with each new generation. Certain gymnasts have played an outsized role in that. Before Olga Korbut arrived, most gymnasts were in their 20s. Their gymnastics was poised and elegant. The 17-year-old Korbut proved very different. At the 1972 Olympics, her daring skills, particularly on uneven bars and balance beam, captured fans' attention. The Soviet star was also charismatic in a way gymnasts had not been before. And she was successful,

Larisa Latynina of the Soviet Union won 14 individual medals and four team medals during her three Olympic appearances.

NOT JUST KIDS

Teenagers have delivered some of history's most famous women's gymnastics performances. Stars don't have to be young, though. The average age of the medalists at the 2021 Olympics was 20.6. And then there's Oksana Chusovitina. Though she didn't medal at those Games, she won a gold and silver in her previous seven Olympics. The Uzbekistani star competed at her eighth Olympics in 2021 at age 46.

winning three gold medals and a silver. Many credit Korbut with beginning the sport's modern era. Her arrival also marked the beginning of a period when younger gymnasts thrived.

That was the world Nadia Comăneci came into at the 1976 Olympics. The 14-year-old Romanian brought new levels of difficulty in her routines. The high-risk aerial moves in her beam routine had never been seen before. Her release move on bars was also a first. And after she scored seven perfect 10s while winning five medals, everyone wanted to follow in her footsteps.

Several countries, including the Soviet Union, boycotted the 1984 Olympics. That opened the door for Mary Lou Retton. The spunky teen from West Virginia shot to stardom with her combination of power and finesse. An enthusiastic home crowd in Los Angeles cheered her every move. In a dramatic finish, Retton sealed the all-around title with a perfect 10 on vault. That made her the first female

US gymnast to win an Olympic medal—and a superstar in her home country.

A new scoring system took effect in 2006, encouraging gymnasts to balance difficulty with execution.

A pair of perfect 10s helped Team USA's Mary Lou Retton secure the women's all-around gold medal at the 1984 Olympics by just .05 points.

Americans thrived. In 2008, the elegant Nastia Liukin held off her more powerful teammate Shawn Johnson to win all-around gold. Gabby Douglas used her dynamic routines to become the sport's first Black all-around champion four years later. And then Simone Biles began rewriting the record books the following year.

DYNASTY

Historically, Russia and Romania were the strongest countries in women's gymnastics. But from 2011 to 2019, nobody could beat the United States. During that time, Team USA won both Olympic gold medals and all five world titles. Americans also won every global all-around title during that span. In fact, US women won every Olympic all-around gold medal from 2004 through 2021. They also won 11 of the 15 world all-around titles from 2005 through 2023.

Though standing under 5 feet tall, Biles is able to generate massive power in her tumbling. This helps her perform eye-popping routines that are packed with difficulty. Yet what truly sets Biles apart is that she also performs with consistency and nearly perfect form. That combination helped her become the most decorated gymnast of all time.

Team USA's Gabby Douglas won three Olympic gold medals over two trips to the Olympic Games.

CHAPTER FIVE

ICONIC MEN

As a soldier for the Soviet Union, Viktor Chukarin was captured during World War II (1939–45). Upon being freed in 1945, he returned to the gym. Finally, in 1952 and at age 30, Chukarin arrived at his first Olympics. Over two appearances in the Games, he won 11 medals. Among his seven gold medals were two in the all-around. Chukarin also helped establish the Soviets as a men's gymnastics power. They were not alone at the top, however.

By the mid-1950s, Japan had emerged as a worthy rival. And after finishing second to the Soviets in 1956, the Japanese men claimed the next five gold medals, holding off the Soviet Union each time. Sawao Katō was a big reason why. A highly disciplined gymnast, he trained hard to perfect his technique. All the while, Katō developed an original style that set him apart from the competition. This led to his

Soviet gymnast Viktor Chukarin's six medals at the 1952 Olympics were the most of any male athlete at the Games.

winning 12 medals over three Olympics. No male gymnast has won more than his eight gold medals. And in 1976, Katō nearly became the first gymnast to win three consecutive Olympic all-around gold medals. However, he fell short by just one point in his final Games.

After the 1952 Olympics, China went 28 years without sending athletes to the Games. They finally returned in 1980. Then, in 1984, Chinese star Li Ning won six medals, including gold on the floor exercise, pommel horse, and rings. That performance helped establish China as a new power in the sport. Li became known as the Prince of Gymnastics in his home country. However, he might be even more famous there for founding a successful athletic apparel and shoe company. The success of his Li-Ning Company has made Li one of the richest people in China.

At the 1992 Olympics, Vitaly Scherbo's six superb routines earned him the all-around title. Then he

TEAM USA

US men have enjoyed occasional success at the Olympics. Bart Conner, Peter Vidmar, and their teammates set the standard in 1984. That group won eight medals, including the country's first team title, while competing on home soil in Los Angeles. In 2004, Paul Hamm became the first US man to win the all-around gold. Danell Leyva later won three medals over two Olympics, including all-around bronze in 2012.

In 2000, Li Ning became the first Chinese athlete inducted into the International Gymnastics Hall of Fame.

kept on going. By the time the Games had finished, the Belarus-born gymnast also won the team, pommel horse, parallel bars, rings, and vault titles. No gymnast had ever won six gold medals in a single Olympics. Three decades later, still no one else had.

The man who became known as King Kōhei began his Olympic career in 2008 with an all-around silver medal. That proved to be the spark Kōhei Uchimura needed to become one of the greatest ever. The Japanese star strived to balance ever-difficult gymnastics with perfect execution. The result was a technically elegant style that had never been seen before. A hugely popular athlete in his home country, Uchimura cruised to all-around Olympic gold medals in 2012 and 2016. But he also added six all-around titles at the World Championships. All told, he won seven Olympic and 21 World Championships medals in a career that will be difficult to match.

Kōhei Uchimura competed in four Olympics for Japan, earning seven medals in the process.

CHAPTER SIX

FLIPPING OUT

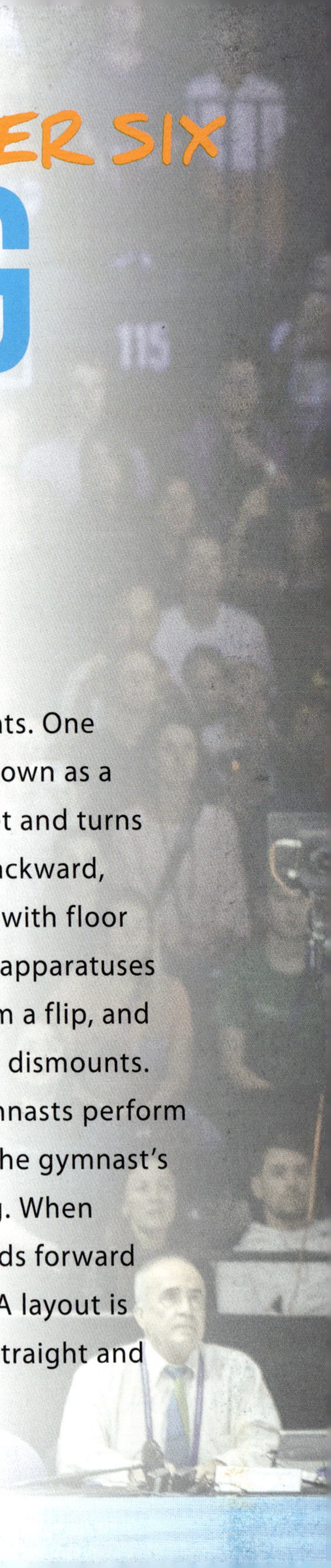

A gymnastics routine includes several elements. One of the most striking skills is the flip. Also known as a salto, this is when the gymnast leaves their feet and turns over completely. Flips can be done forward, backward, or sideways. Though flips are most connected with floor exercise and vault, they can be done on other apparatuses too. On the bars, a gymnast can let go, perform a flip, and grab the bar again. Flips are also often used in dismounts.

There are four basic positions in which gymnasts perform flips. The most basic is the tuck. This is when the gymnast's knees are pulled into their body while flipping. When flipping in the pike position, the gymnast bends forward at the waist while keeping their legs straight. A layout is a flip in which the gymnast keeps their body straight and

Harry Hepworth of Great Britain flips in a tuck position off the vault at the 2023 World Championships.

extended, with their legs together. When flipping in a straddle position, the gymnast keeps their legs straight but split apart.

As gymnasts become more advanced, they can add difficulty to their saltos. One way to do this is by adding additional flips. Double back flips are common in elite floor exercise routines. Gymnasts typically perform them as part of a tumbling pass that begins with a roundoff and back handspring. When someone says "double back," they're usually referring to a tuck. A double back pike carries the same difficulty value as a double back tuck. However, a double back layout has a higher value.

Another way to make flips more difficult is by adding twists. A full-twisting double back includes two back flips with a 360-degree spin. Especially good tumblers can incorporate two or even three full twists into a double back.

STICK THE LANDING

One of the most important parts of a routine is the dismount. The goal is to stick the landing. This means the gymnast's feet hit the mat in a controlled manner, like they're sticking to the mat. A gymnast who hops or steps when landing has points taken off from their score. A proper stick is about more than just the feet. First, the gymnast must be fully rotated and in control. Then, to absorb the impact, the gymnast should land with bent knees and their arms pointing forward for balance.

Back flips are more common than front flips because they are generally easier to perform. One common forward-facing flip is called the double Arabian. In this move, the gymnast begins like they're going to do a back flip, but then they quickly turn 180 degrees and flip forward twice.

Adding twists and spins to flips can earn competitors higher scores if they are executed correctly.

CHAPTER SEVEN

NAME THAT SKILL

The FIG Code of Points outlines the rules and scoring for each level of gymnastics. When an elite gymnast performs a brand-new skill in a major competition, such as the Olympics, the skill is named for that gymnast.

Gymnastics fans would recognize many of these skills. The Tkachev is a difficult release move on high bar or uneven bars. To perform it, the gymnast travels backward over the bar before grabbing it again. The skill was named for Soviet gymnast Alexandr Tkachev in 1977.

Hungary's Henrietta Ónodi introduced her namesake balance beam skill in 1989. It's an elegant move combining a backward jump into a forward walkover. Canada's Victoria Moors completed a double-twisting, double back layout on floor exercise in 2013. It's now called the Moors. Many of the

Nastia Liukin of the United States prepares to grab the bar and complete a Tkachev at the 2008 Olympics in Beijing, China.

best women's vaulters perform the ultra-difficult Cheng. It's named for former Chinese star Cheng Fei.

Svetlana Khorkina of Russia at one point had eight named skills. However, some were later removed from the Code of Points. Nellie Kim now holds the record with seven named skills. The former Soviet star's skills came on three different events.

YURCHENKO

Perhaps the most famous named skill is the Yurchenko on vault. Historically gymnasts approached the apparatus facing forward. Natalia Yurchenko had a different idea. At a meet in 1982, the Soviet star performed a roundoff onto the springboard. Then she did a back handspring onto the vault table. Today the roundoff entry is the most common technique for elite gymnasts.

In recent years, no gymnast has pushed the limits of the sport more than Simone Biles. The American got her first named skill in 2013, on floor exercise. But her boundary-pushing gymnastics really turned heads in 2019. That year, she performed a double-twisting, double back tuck dismount on balance beam. And on floor, she landed another double-twisting, double back tuck. Both skills had been previously unthinkable. Then, four years later, she performed a roundoff double pike on vault that's so difficult few men dare attempt it. But like so many of Biles's five named skills, she managed to make it look easy.

Because Simone Biles performed two original moves on vault, the first is called the Biles, while the second is called the Biles II.

CHAPTER EIGHT

COLLEGE GYMNASTICS

A sellout crowd of more than 9,000 fans turned Auburn Arena into a sea of orange. And now they were on their feet, all eyeing the balance beam. Six months earlier, Sunisa Lee had won the Olympic women's all-around gold medal in Tokyo, Japan. Now the Minnesotan was here as a freshman gymnast for the Auburn Tigers, ready to perform in a meet against rival Alabama.

Women have been competing in college gymnastics since the late 1960s. The National Collegiate Athletic Association (NCAA) began holding a national championship in 1982. In the years since, women's gymnastics has grown to become one of the most popular college sports. Former elite superstars such as Lee are a big reason why. Against Alabama, Lee moved through her difficult beam routine with ease. She ended her electric performance by sticking the landing. Lee's 9.975 proved to be the meet's highest score.

Sunisa Lee was the 2021–22 NCAA champion on the balance beam. She also finished second in the all-around competition.

Yet Lee's star power was only part of the appeal that night. College gymnastics is a big show. Upon finishing her beam routine, Lee flashed a bright smile and ran to her joyous teammates. The crowd in Auburn Arena roared. It's no wonder why they were having fun. Lee not only won the all-around, but her big scores also helped the Tigers beat Alabama for only the third time ever.

"We felt like we had something to prove, and I think we did exactly that," Lee said. "We enjoyed every single moment."

Elite gymnastics is intense and individual. The college version of the sport is very different. Gymnasts emphasize the team over the individual. They loudly cheer on one another at meets. And though the level of gymnastics isn't as difficult as in elite competitions, the less rigorous training allows athletes to compete more often. They're also able to show off their personalities more.

COLLEGE MEN

College men's gymnastics has a rich history of its own. The first NCAA title was awarded in 1938. Schools such as Illinois, Oklahoma, Penn State, and Stanford have enjoyed much success. And over the years, many gymnasts have gone on from college teams to make the Olympics. That included all five members of the US team in 2021. However, the sport has struggled to match the success of women's college gymnastics. As of 2024, only 12 teams remained in the men's top division.

This, in turn, helps some performances go viral even outside the gymnastics community.

More and more elite gymnasts are electing to continue their careers in college. Lee became the first Olympic

While competing for UCLA in 2019, Katelyn Ohashi's perfect 10 floor routine went viral, gaining more than 200 million views on the university's athletics YouTube channel.

In 2023, women's gymnastics was one of six NCAA championships to draw 1 million television viewers.

all-around champion to do so. But she was hardly the first Olympian to compete in college. In fact, three of her Olympic teammates also competed in the 2023 college season. One other had wrapped up her college career before the Games. Many Olympians from other countries also compete for US colleges.

At the core of college gymnastics, however, are the teams. Utah was the sport's first power. The team nicknamed the Red Rocks won the first five NCAA titles. Through 2023, their nine total championships trailed only Georgia, which had 10. Alabama, Oklahoma, and UCLA each had at least six. Certain teams develop unique styles or personalities. And when they meet on the competition floor, fans don't want to look away.

CHAPTER NINE

AMAZING MOMENTS

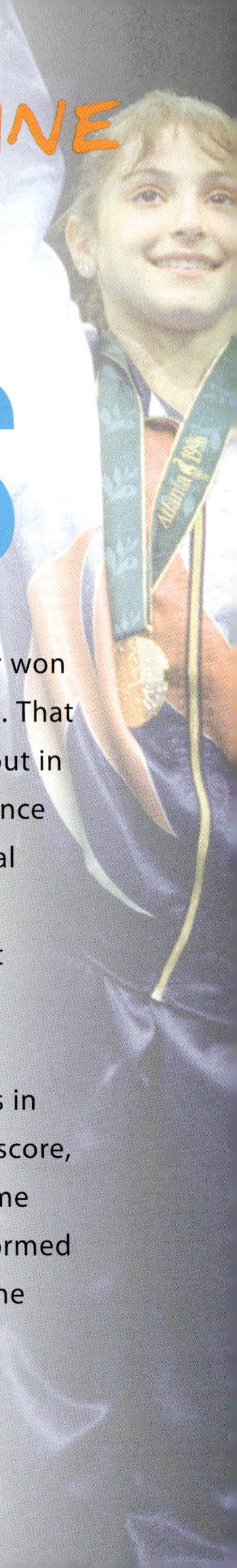

Entering the 1996 Games, the United States had never won an Olympic team gold medal in women's gymnastics. That looked like it could change as the competition played out in Atlanta. The US women put themselves in striking distance of the gold. All they needed was to succeed in their final rotation, on vault. That's when disaster struck.

Dominique Moceanu, Team USA's youngest gymnast at just 14, fell on both of her vault attempts. Then the Americans' final gymnast, Kerri Strug, fell on her first attempt as well. Even worse, the landing tore ligaments in her left ankle. But believing the team needed a higher score, Strug returned to the runway to try again. With the home crowd roaring, she charged through the pain and performed a Yurchenko with 1 1/2 twists. Amazingly, Strug stuck the landing, keeping most of her weight on her right foot.

Kerri Strug wore a walking boot on the medal stand after her courageous effort on the vault secured the gold medal for the United States in 1996.

SVETLANA KHORKINA

Svetlana Khorkina of Russia was gymnastics' biggest star during the late 1990s and early 2000s. The 2000 Olympics did not go as planned. A favorite to win all-around gold, she fell on vault. It was later revealed the vault had been set to the wrong height. This affected several gymnasts. Khorkina did her best to move on. She found some redemption a few days later. Taller than most gymnasts, she packed her uneven bars routine with original skills. And in the bars final, she nailed her routine to win a second consecutive gold medal in the event.

After saluting the judges, she collapsed to the mat in pain. The gutsy vault ensured Team USA won the gold medal. It's lived on as one of the most iconic performances in Olympic history.

Fans are drawn to gymnastics for a variety of reasons. Some love the artistry and athleticism. Others are taken in by the dramatic performances. Whatever the reason, the sport has provided many captivating moments over the years.

Going into the 1976 Olympics, Japan's men had won four consecutive gold medals. Few expected Shun Fujimoto to be the key to a fifth. Japan began the team final on floor. That's when Fujimoto landed awkwardly on a tumbling pass and shattered his kneecap. Still, knowing his team needed him, Fujimoto fought through two more routines. The latter was on rings, where his dismount required a hard landing.

In addition to their five straight Olympic team gold medals from 1960 to 1976, Japan's men also won the team competition in 2004 and 2016.

Fujimoto not only managed it, but he posted his best score ever on the event. The injury proved too painful to continue after that. But Fujimoto's famous performance proved key in Japan claiming its record-setting fifth consecutive gold medal.

Other moments stand out for their incredible execution. At the 2012 Olympics, the US women opened with a stunning round of vaults. No one shined as bright as McKayla Maroney. Her ultra-difficult Amanar included a Yurchenko entry, followed by 2 1/2 twists. Maroney soared so high, and with such perfect form, that even the judges were visibly awed. That vault helped propel the Americans to their first gold medal in 16 years.

McKayla Maroney's vault in the 2012 Olympic team competition earned the highest score of any performance at that year's Games.

CHAPTER TEN

MORE DISCIPLINES

When thinking of gymnastics, most people think of artistic gymnastics. After all, it's the most popular gymnastics discipline, with famous athletes competing at the collegiate and Olympic level. Yet gymnastics includes more than just that discipline. In fact, two others are included in the Olympics.

Rhythmic gymnastics became an Olympic sport in 1984. It shares some similarities with artistic gymnastics, including the basic scoring. However, there are also key differences. Rhythmic gymnasts perform routines using one of four hand-held apparatuses: ribbon, hoop, ball, and clubs. In each routine, the gymnast uses a different apparatus in an expressive performance set to music. The best athletes demonstrate skill, flexibility, and an ability to relate their performance to the music.

Rhythmic gymnast Dina Averina of Russia performs a clubs routine at the Olympic games in Tokyo, Japan, in July 2021.

At the Olympics, rhythmic gymnastics is a women-only sport. It was the only such sport approved for the 2024 Olympics. In the individual all-around event, gymnasts perform four routines, each with a different apparatus. It follows the same basic format as in artistic gymnastics. There is also a group event. This consists of two routines. In the first, all five gymnasts perform together using the same apparatus. Next, the gymnasts perform together while split between two apparatuses. Traditionally, athletes from countries in Eastern Europe have dominated the rhythmic gymnastics events.

A STUNNING UPSET

No country comes close to Russia when it comes to Olympic medals in rhythmic gymnastics. Twin sisters Dina and Arina Averina, representing the Russian Olympic Committee, were favorites to win more in 2021. Neither ended up with the gold, though. Instead, Linoy Ashram of Israel shocked fans by beating them both. It was only the third Olympic gold medal in Israel's history, and the first by an Israeli woman.

Trampoline gymnastics has been part of the Olympics since 2000. In this sport, athletes perform dizzying combinations of flips and spins while jumping on large trampolines. Each jump can be upwards of 25 feet (7.6 m) in the air. While airborne, the gymnast must perform forward and backward skills. Canada's Rosie MacLennan became the first trampolinist to win back-to-back Olympic titles, doing so in 2012 and 2016. But going into 2024, Chinese gymnasts had twice as many trampoline medals as any other country.

Rosie MacLennan served as the flag bearer for Team Canada at the 2016 Olympics before taking home her second straight gold in trampoline gymnastics.

Outside of the Olympics, trampoline competitions also include other events. In synchronized trampoline, two gymnasts perform identical routines on side-by-side trampolines. Double-mini trampoline routines have two jumps. The gymnast charges down a runway, bounces off one trampoline, and then a second, before landing on a mat. In each jump, they perform high-flying skills. Tumbling gymnastics also takes place on a runway. In each routine, athletes perform eight tumbling elements, with the final one ending on a thicker pad.

Athletes can also compete internationally in acrobatic gymnastics and parkour events. In acrobatics routines, gymnasts work together in routines set to music. Skills include holds, lifts, throws, and tumbling. Parkour athletes perform freestyle moves over obstacles on a course. Some events are judged on creativity, while others are races.

The first acrobatic gymnastics world championships were held in 1974.

CHAPTER ELEVEN

WELLNESS

Gymnastics can be a demanding sport. Athletes push themselves to the limits, mentally and physically. The quest to achieve perfection can be motivating. However, without proper training and support, gymnasts can face an increased risk of injury or other problems.

Strong gymnastics starts with proper nutrition. Gymnasts who are fully fueled perform at a higher level, recover faster, and sleep better. Experts at the US Olympic & Paralympic Committee recommend gymnasts eat a balanced diet high in vegetables, grains, and lean proteins. In addition to eating the right foods, gymnasts must eat enough food. Not getting enough nutrients can lead to fatigue, poor bone health, or other problems. Because of this, coaches are moving away from the outdated practice of weighing gymnasts, which can lead to an overemphasis on weight. Instead, athletes should focus on maintaining their overall health.

In addition, rest and recovery are needed for gymnasts to be at their best. That includes mental rest. "Sometimes we only focus on the negatives, and it's hard to see the

Simone Biles helped bring increased awareness to mental wellness in gymnastics after struggling with a condition called "the twisties" at the 2021 Olympic Games in Tokyo, Japan.

positives," said Ellie Black, a three-time Olympian from Canada. So, if she has a hard day of training, Black makes a point of finding positives. For example, a bad routine in training helps her prepare if a routine doesn't go as planned in competition.

Unfortunately, the intense nature of gymnastics has allowed abusive cultures to form. For many years, people believed extreme coaching techniques were needed to reach a championship level. Many in the sport are working to change that. In recent years, more and more athletes have spoken out about their negative experiences. This has led to important changes meant to protect the athletes. Still, if a gymnast feels uncomfortable or at risk of injury in practice, they should talk to a parent or another trusted adult outside of the gym.

Gymnastics is an incredibly challenging sport.

SLEEP IT OFF

Aly Raisman became one of the United States' most decorated gymnasts during the 2010s. She won three medals, including two golds, at the 2012 Olympics. Then she added three more medals, including another gold, in 2016. One of the keys to her comeback was getting enough sleep. "Everyone calls her 'Grandma Aly' because she goes to bed (early) and takes a lot of naps and sleeps a lot and is just, you know, a health nut," joked her Olympic teammate Gabby Douglas.

When performed safely and in a positive environment, it can also be fulfilling. In the right atmosphere, athletes can learn exciting skills, make new friends, and achieve things they never thought possible.

Ellie Black represented Canada at three straight Olympic Games starting in 2012.

GLOSSARY

apparatus
A piece of equipment that is used in gymnastics.

boycott
Refusing to purchase a product or take part in an event as a form of protest.

charismatic
Having a charming quality that draws people in.

dismount
The move in which a gymnast leaves the apparatus to finish a routine.

evolve
To grow or change.

generation
A group of people who are similar in age and other identifying characteristics.

handspring
An acrobatic move in which a person jumps onto their hands and then continues on until landing back on their feet.

iconic
Well-known for excellence.

rival
An opponent with whom a player or team has a fierce and ongoing competition.

routine
A set performance by a gymnast on one apparatus.

tumbling
Elements such as flips and handsprings.

viral
Spreading quickly across social media.

MORE INFORMATION

Books

Flynn, Brendan. *Girls' Gymnastics*. Abdo, 2022.

Lawrence, Blythe. *Best Male Gymnasts of All Time*. Abdo, 2021.

Martinson, Morgan. *Suni Lee*. Abdo, 2022.

Online Resources

Booklinks
NONFICTION NETWORK
FREE! ONLINE NONFICTION RESOURCES

To learn more about gymnastics, please visit **abdobooklinks.com** or scan this QR code. These links are routinely monitored and updated to provide the most current information available.

INDEX

About the Author

Chrös McDougall is a sportswriter, author, and book editor who focuses on Olympic and Paralympic sports. After reporting on the women's college gymnastics team at the University of Missouri, he has covered the sport's elite level for more than a decade, including at the 2008 and 2020 Olympics. His work appears on TeamUSA.com and other outlets. McDougall lives in Minneapolis, Minnesota, with his wife, two children, and a distinctly inelegant boxer named Eira.